CW00739871

The Topiary Garden

JM

JANNI HOWKER

The Topiary Garden

WITH PICTURES BY

ANTHONY BROWNE

Julia MacRae Books

LONDON SYDNEY AUCKLAND JOHANNESBURG

Text © 1984, 1993 Janni Howker

Illustrations © 1993 A.E.T. Browne & Partners

All rights reserved

THE TOPIARY GARDEN
was first published in 1984 by Julia MacRae Books
in *Badger on the Barge*, a collection
of stories by Janni Howker

This edition first published in Great Britain 1993 by
Julia MacRae

An imprint of the Random House Group
20 Vauxhall Bridge Road, London SW1V 2SA

Random House Australia (Pty) Ltd
20 Alfred Street, Milsons Point, Sydney, NSW 2061

Random House New Zealand Ltd
18 Poland Road, Glenfield, Auckland, New Zealand

Random House South Africa (Pty) Ltd
PO Box 337, Bergvlei 2012, South Africa

Designed by Douglas Martin

Printed in Hong Kong

British Library Cataloguing in Publication Data
A catalogue record for this book is available from
the British Library

ISBN 1–85681–111–5

For Hannah

1

LIZ RAN. "It's not fair!" she yelled. "It's not fair!" And she dashed from the camp site into the lane.

The shadows of the trees striped her, and between them flashed the gables and chimneys of Carlton Hall with the disc of the sun spinning on the tower like a blazing weathervane. Her chest was bursting with anger and her eyes stung as if they had soap in them.

At last she could not run any further. The lane was too steep. She dropped down onto the grass by the dry-stone wall and huddled there for a long time with the new sketch-book clutched in her hands. Dad shouldn't have laughed! He should have belted Alan! He shouldn't have laughed!

Far down the hill she could hear him calling her name, looking for her. Jackdaws circled the chimneys of the Hall. A skylark drifted down the warm evening sky like the ghost of a parachutist. Dad stopped calling and the quietness was all around her.

She rubbed her stinging eyes until sparks came, but she was too angry to cry. An evening breeze hushed through the trees and the leaf shadows swished over her. The sparks faded from her eyes, and she opened her book. On the inside cover Mrs Metcalf had written in beautiful black letters –

PRESENTED TO ELIZABETH JACKSON FOR GOOD WORK IN ART. But on the first page Alan had drawn a crude sketch of the body of a naked woman, graffiti-style – just a body with no head or arms or legs, in red felt-tip pen. Underneath, he had scribbled *Nude by Alan Michelangelo Jackson!*

Alan was her elder brother. And the small sketchbook, with its green cover and expensive white paper, was the first thing Liz had ever won in her life. The sparks came back to her eyes. She ripped the page out of the book, screwed it up into a ball and shoved it deep into a crack in the wall. Then, much more carefully, she tried to tear out the ragged edge of paper, which meant she had to take out the back page as well. She screwed that up too. She would not let him spoil her prize.

But even though the pages were clean again, she knew that in some way he had. And she knew that if she did not draw something in the book now, this minute, she never would. It would be spoiled forever, because of what Alan had done, and because Dad had laughed.

She took the new pencil out of her back pocket. With quick angry lines she drew a figure running. Underneath, she wrote: *She went away, far away, and never came back.* In the sky above the running figure she drew three black birds, which were the rooks she could see trailing back to the trees. Now some of the anger was on the page, and less of it was inside her.

Again the breeze swished the leaves of the beech trees, and now the sun had gone down behind the tower of the Hall. The sky was streaked with purple and red.

Putting the sketchbook into the back pocket of her jeans, Liz walked quickly on, away from the ruined pages in the wall, and away from the caravan where they were staying. But she knew she would have to go back sometime.

Only the figure in her book could keep running, far, far, over the hills.

It was getting darker now, and a pale moon, like a white snail shell, had crept up the sky. Where a gate opened off the lane into a field, Liz stopped, leaned on the gate post, and stared down into the valley. The first lights flickered on the camp site. She was waiting for Dad to call her again, so that she could pretend not to hear him.

The strangeness of being able to see so far calmed more of the anger from her. At home, in Mill Street, all you could see was the Co-Op and the houses across the road. Here, distant fells smoked and darkened on the horizon. A bat flickered under the branches of the trees, weaving an invisible web. The shadows crept together across the lane, until they were not shadows but a blue darkness. The moon brightened. Liz saw the white scut of a rabbit's tail as it hopped across the dewy grass. She held her breath to watch. The stillness over the countryside was like a very distant sound.

Suddenly the rabbit fled, zig-zagging back to the cover of the wall, startling her. An instant later she heard the munch of footsteps on the stony lane.

A figure came over the slope, leaning on a stick, with the moon on its hunched shoulder.

Liz suddenly felt a long way from the caravan. She stayed very still.

"Evening, lass." It was the voice of an old woman carrying through the quiet air.

"Hello," answered Liz with relief, as the stranger reached her.

"Red at night," said the old woman, jerking her chin towards the last streaks of pink behind the Hall.

Liz stared at her. It looked more like an old man who was standing there in the dark lane, thin and stooping and leaning on a stick, because the woman was wearing a long brown coat tied at the waist with a bit of rope, a pair of black wellies, and, on her head, a cloth cap, like the old men in Mill Street wore. "Pardon?" said Liz politely.

"Red at night,
Shepherd's delight. Should be a grand day tomorrow."

"Oh," said Liz. "My dad'll be pleased. The trials are tomorrow."

"You're here for that, are you?"

"Yes. Dad's in it." Liz fell into step by the stranger. It would be better walking back under the dark whispering branches of the trees with someone else.

"Do you live here?" she asked after a moment, because it seemed rather rude to say nothing when you walked next to someone.

The old woman walked very slowly, with her nose pointing at the ground and her thin shoulders up round her ears. "Aye. Down there. Yew Tree Cottage. Opposite the topiary garden." Her voice was dry and rattling. "Sally Beck's the name."

"I'm Liz," said Liz.

They walked in silence for a time, with only the sound of their shoes slowly crunching the stones, and the dull tap of Sally Beck's stick.

Liz knew that really she should hurry back to the camp site. Dad would be getting worried. Serves him right! she thought.

"And what's it like, being young these days?" asked the old woman suddenly, glancing sideways at her from the shadow of her cap.

"I don't know," said Liz, surprised. "I've never been anything else!"

Sally Beck chuckled quietly, and gave her stick an extra tap on the ground. Her coat made a swishing sound round her boots as she walked. And the sound was like her laugh.

"Only," said Liz, thoughtfully chewing the end of her plait, and half speaking to herself, "I wish I was a boy sometimes . . ."

Sally Beck stopped still. And once more the moon stopped behind her shoulder, blue and bright, and not quite a full circle. "Do you now? Now there's a funny thing. I was a boy once upon a time – oh yes, yes I was."

"A boy!" said Liz, staring at her.

"Liz! Lizzy!" her dad was running up the lane towards them. "Where the heck have you been?"

"Come to the Yews. I'll tell you," said Sally Beck. "If you're interested." And she stepped through a gap in the wall and vanished among the trees. Liz gazed after her, until she had gone into the darkness.

"Oh! There you are!" cried Dad. "It was only a joke, Liz.

He didn't mean anything."

"What?" said Liz.

"Alan's halfway up Carlton Fell looking for you! He didn't mean to upset you like that." Dad's voice sounded loud in the quiet lane. "You daft tuppence! You might have got lost." He put his arm round Liz's shoulder.

Liz remembered her anger, and shook him off. She walked stiffly ahead of him all the way to the caravan.

"Dad!" said Alan, running towards them across the field. "I can't find her anywhere."

"She's here," said Dad. "Now say you're sorry."

"Sorry, Liz."

"Sod you!" said Liz quietly, as Dad went round the back of the van to turn on the gas-bottle.

"Hoy! It was just a joke!" Alan was four years older than Liz, and too big to hit.

"And not a very funny one at that," said Dad, unzipping the awning.

"You laughed!" cried Liz, accusingly.

"Well, that doesn't mean I thought it was funny," said Dad, lying. "Now give over, you two. Don't spoil our weekend, eh?"

The small caravan smelt of the musty canvas and the hot fumes of petrol and oil from Dad's trials-bike which he had put in the awning for safety. Alan was going to sleep next to it, to make sure no one nicked it, or knobbled it, because the first heat of the Carlton Hall Trials Event was tomorrow, and the prize, if Dad won, was a hundred pounds.

Liz dropped down onto her narrow bunk bed, as Dad put

a match to the hissing gas-mantles. The light in the caravan suddenly made it pitch black outside.

"Come on, our Lizzy. Put the kettle on," said Dad.

"Shan't."

"Now look what you've done, Alan. You've upset the cook! There goes our bacon butties for the weekend!" Dad laughed, and put the kettle on himself.

"Hey, Liz," said Alan, his leather jacket creaking as he pulled it off. "Did Dad tell you – there's going to be a Fancy Dress Barbecue on Sunday night." He was smiling at her, trying to make friends again.

Liz shrugged.

"What are you going to go as?" Dad hunted for mugs in the cupboard.

"Dunno yet," said Alan. "Perhaps we could go as Laurel and Hardy." He glanced at Liz. But she wouldn't look at him. "Unless our Lizzy can think of something."

"Sounds like a good idea," said Dad. "And Liz could go as . . ." he tapped his fingers on the table, trying to think of something. Then he snapped his finger and thumb. "Got it! Liz could go as an artist! You could wear one of my shirts back to front for a smock, and Alan's scarf for a floppy bow tie. And we could make you a pointed beard and a moustache out of cardboard, and one of those palette things."

"Yeh! Great!" said Alan. "You'd look really great!"

Their enthusiasm made Liz feel a bit sick. The sparks came back over her eyes. "Not all artists are men!" she snapped.

"Course they are," said Alan. "Picasso, Michelangelo-er-um-Leonardo da Vinci. Go on then, tell us a woman artist." He was standing in front of her, very cocky, and angry because she wouldn't make friends and forgive him.

Liz opened her mouth. Then shut it again. She was sure there were some women artists, but she could not think of a single name.

The corner of Alan's mouth drew down in a little triumphant grin.

"Sally Beck!" said Liz. It was a lie. It was the first name that came into her head. It was the name of the old woman she had met.

Alan looked at her suspiciously. "Never heard of her."

"Oh, I have," said Dad breezily, stirring the tea. He did not know anything about art or artists. He was just trying to make peace. "Very famous. Isn't she, Liz?"

Liz grinned. "Very, very famous," she said.

Alan shrugged. "I still think Dad's idea was good, anyhow."

"Come on, bed, both of you," said Dad, before another squabble broke out.

Liz pulled the curtain round the bunk, so that her bed was like a narrow tent. She crawled into her sleeping bag, with her sketchbook and pencil, and her tin of coloured crayons.

"She went away, far away, and never came back," she read to herself in a whisper, as she shaded in the darkness of the sky and the hill with blue and purple and pink.

Then she turned to the next white page and drew two

figures standing under a tree and the moon sitting in the branches like an owl. She thought for a long moment, then she wrote: *And she met a stranger who said Red at night is my delight for I was a boy once upon a time.*

And writing the words made a prickly feeling run all along her arms and up to the back of her neck.

"Finished your tea, love?" said Dad, lifting the edge of the curtain.

Liz quickly closed her book.

"Yes, thanks."

"Night, then. Sleep tight, and remember to say a prayer for your mam." Dad had said that every night since Liz was four, when her mam had died.

"Night, Dad," said Liz, as he let the curtain drop. She heard the buzz of Dad's and Alan's voices in the awning, talking about the motorbike and the competition tomorrow. She opened the sketchbook and looked at the two pictures she had drawn.

What Alan had done didn't matter now – at least, not much. Because she had a secret. In her book she was in a strange story, and tomorrow, perhaps, she'd find out what would happen next. Liz was always the figure in her pictures – the small figure with thin arms and legs and two long brown plaits.

PRESENTED TO ELIZABETH JACKSON FOR GOOD WORK. She traced the words proudly with the tip of her finger. "You've got a very distinctive style, Elizabeth," Mrs Metcalf had said when she had given her the prize. "It's a gift. I hope you'll use this sketchbook to develop it over the summer."

Liz smiled to herself. Sally Beck! she thought, and almost laughed out loud. But she made a mental note to ask Mrs Metcalf the names of some real women artists when she got back to school.

She slipped the sketchbook under her pillow and closed her eyes. "Our Father, God bless Dad, and our mam who art in heaven," she murmured dutifully. "And," she added, "make our Alan fall on his face in some mud, Amen."

Then she lay, listening to Dad's voice buzzing on the caravan windows like a brown bee. Somewhere in the moon-blue gardens of Carlton Hall an owl hooted. She fell asleep, thinking of the strange thing the old woman had said.

2

"THAT LAD in the white caravan fancies you, Liz," said Alan, next morning, grinning at her over his bacon butty.

"Shut up," said Liz, turning her own bacon over in the frying pan with a fork. Alan was always saying stupid things like that, trying to embarrass her.

"Hoy, Dad!" said Alan, still grinning, as Dad came in from the awning wiping his hands on an oily rag. "That lad fancies our Liz. He's been watching her ever since she went to the tap."

Dad glanced out of the caravan window. "Well, he isn't watching her now. He's watching that idiot Johnson showing off on his bike." A black line appeared between Dad's eyebrows. He shoved the rag into his pocket and strode back out of the van as a motorbike roared past the awning.

"Can't you blooming read!" they heard him yell. "Hoy! Johnson! I'm talking to you!"

There was a sign at the gate of the field which read: *No bikes to be ridden on the camp site!* That was the rule Carlton Hall had imposed when they rented the field for the competitors to use. The motorbike puttered to a stop, and a moment later Dad came back in, making the caravan rock.

"Idiot! It only takes one to spoil it for the rest of us."

"What did he say?" Alan poured a dollop of tomato sauce onto his bread.

"Nothing I'd repeat before a lady," said Dad, and smiled at Liz. "Anyhow, I told him the marshals would disqualify anyone who broke the rule. That stopped him."

Alan twisted round on the bunk so that he could look out of the window. "Look at him! Showing off in his fancy leathers – just like a big wet girl!"

Liz glared at the bacon which was still spitting in the pan. "Shut up!" she said.

"Now what's the matter?" Dad pulled on his black boot. He glanced up at her.

"Him! Saying that!"

"Saying what?" said Alan, blinking at her.

"Saying that about him showing off like a . . ."

"That's enough! I've just about had enough of you two squabbling!" said Dad, stamping his foot into the boot and yanking up the zip. He held out his hand. His fingernails were black-rimmed with oil. "The palm of this hand is getting very itchy. Very, very itchy. Understand?"

Alan shrugged and glared at Liz. Liz scowled and let the bacon burn. "It isn't fair," she muttered under her breath.

"Anyhow," said Alan. "It's just a saying. It doesn't mean anything."

"Yes, it does!"

"Lii-iiz!" Dad hissed her name, warningly.

"It isn't fair," said Liz again. And went to eat her bacon out on the grass. Alan was always saying stupid things about girls, but no one apart from her seemed to notice.

It was going to be a warm day – already the sun was high in the sky. The field was like a fairground. There were glittering motorbikes by every caravan, and trucks and trailers. Lines of chequered red and white flags were strung from poles by the gate, and between the poles was a big cloth banner: CARLTON HALL TRIALS EVENT SAT JULY 25TH – SUN JULY 26TH – and in smaller letters underneath: *Sponsored by Stoughton's Pale Ale*. Clumps of men and boys in bright leathers or black leather jackets flashing with badges, stood round the bikes. The smell of cooking bacon mingled with the smell of petrol across the field. A group of little kids played round the tap near the wall, yelling and splashing up a glittering spray of water.

Through the trees across the road the old chimneys and gables stood darkly, indifferent to all of it. While up on Carlton Fell, where the trials were to take place, a motorbike buzzed like a chain saw.

Liz looked round for someone to make friends with, but she couldn't even see another girl, apart from the little child by the tap, and an older girl who didn't count because her boyfriend had his arm round her shoulder and was kissing her ear. The fringe on the sleeve of his leather jacket hung down her back.

Alan came out of the awning, wheeling Dad's bike. She could tell by the look on his face that he was pretending it belonged to him. And he was wearing an old pair of Dad's motorbike boots. The buckles jinked like spurs.

"Nice bike," said the lad from the white caravan, sauntering across.

"Not bad," said Alan, dead casual, and swung himself astride it. He pretended to be doing something with the throttle.

"Won anything?"

Liz saw Alan hesitate.

"It's me Dad's actually," he had to admit, seeing her watching him.

The lad crouched to inspect the silver intestines of the engine. "Oh, I thought it was yours."

Alan smiled, pressing his lips together, very pleased. "I ride it sometimes," he said.

Liz stared at the grass between her sandals, plucked an aimless handful and tossed it away. That's what it would be like all day, she thought. Alan and Dad talking to other competitors about pistons and points and what sort of tyre tread was best, while she'd wander round, until at some point she'd find herself with the wives and girlfriends, making sandwiches and coffee for the marshals, or looking after the little kids. It wasn't much of a way to spend your summer holiday – but that was how they had spent it ever since she could remember. Trials and scrambles and races, year after year.

Alan and the other lad had gone off together to look at another bike. Dad ducked out of the awning, looking like a cross between a diver and a spaceman in his red and black leathers. He grinned at her.

"Going to draw a picture of your old dad on his metal donkey?" he said, coming to sit by her on the grass. His leathers creaked round his knees and elbows.

[22]

"I don't like drawing bikes," said Liz. But she thought he looked handsome in his gear, and quite young for a dad. Some of the men looked like the Michelin-tyre man in theirs.

Dad's grin slipped away, and he looked at her thoughtfully. "It's not much fun for you any more, is it Liz?"

Liz plucked another handful of grass.

"It wasn't so bad when you were little like them." He looked at the gaggle of small kids who were stamping through the puddle they had made.

"It's alright," said Liz. But it wasn't really. "Do I have to come up to the fell?" She wanted to go and find the old woman.

"Don't you want to watch me win?"

"Yes. But . . ." She felt mean.

"Well," said Dad. "I suppose you're old enough to be sensible. But don't go far from the camp site."

"I thought I could go and look at the Hall, or something."

"I'll leave you a key for the van – make sure you lock up properly though."

Alan and his new friend came over to them. "Dad, can I go up the fell with Mike and his brother?"

Mike was carrying two helmets by their straps.

"Aye, alright. But don't you go messing about." Dad got to his feet, and tossed Liz the spare caravan key. "I want you both back here for tea – and Lizzy, don't go talking to any strange men."

"They'd have to be strange to talk to our Lizzy!" cried Alan.

[23]

Liz put her tongue out at him as far as it would go.

Even in the wood Liz could still hear the intermittent growl of the trials-bikes up on the fell. Now the field next to the camp site was full of cars, and a policeman was standing in the lane, wearing white gloves to direct the traffic and the spectators.

Just for a moment Liz thought about turning back. Sometimes it was good to be among the crowd, knowing your dad was in the competition. It gave you a sort of superior feeling. But she could feel the hard edges of her sketchbook in her pocket, and she knew that today she wanted to be in a story of her own – and not be a spectator on the edge of Dad's and Alan's adventures.

Among the trees the light was green and cool like water, and full of the peppery scents of ferns and brambles. Birds twittered drowsily, making the wood seem very still. She found a path which ran at the foot of a high stone wall, beyond which, she guessed, would lie the Hall gardens.

There was something secret about being in the green leafy stillness between the wood and the wall. It was a place for imagining things. But the only trouble was, the harder she tried to pretend something was about to happen, the less certain she became that she really had met the old woman last night in the lane who had said such a strange thing.

Stopping in a patch of sunlight, she took out her book and looked again at the picture she had drawn. "I was a boy once upon a time". It sounded a bit daft – and besides, it didn't seem very likely. She chewed thoughtfully at the end of one of her plaits, then flicked it back over her shoulder.

The wall led her round to the front of the Hall where there were a pair of tall wrought-iron gates with gold-tipped spikes. One of the gates stood open, and on the other was a sign: CARLTON HALL. GARDENS OPEN TO THE PUBLIC APRIL–OCTOBER. CHILDREN MUST BE ACCOMPANIED BY AN ADULT.

Beyond the gates was the strangest garden Liz had ever seen – all hedges and yew trees cut into cones and mush-rooms, spires and pyramids, like shapes carved out of green pumice stone. Behind them was the Hall itself, grey and formal as a church. One or two couples strolled among the dense green hedges and a man stood with his back to her taking a photograph of a bush clipped to look like a peacock.

Liz decided to ignore the sign – if anyone asked, she'd pretend to be looking for her dad. She slipped through the open gate into the quietness of the garden.

She passed through an archway in a tall green wall. Another plaque was set in the gravel. "The topiary garden," she read, "was created in 1721 by Sir Randolph Chadwick for the pleasure of his wife."

The green battlements enclosed a secret path, over which loomed the black shapes of the topiary against the bright sky. It was like being among huge chessmen, Liz thought, as she walked slowly among the clipped bushes and trees. She came to a place in the heart of the topiary garden where there was a small, perfectly round lawn, upon which stood a marble statue of a nude woman. Her arms were broken off just above the elbow. And all round her stood black yews

[25]

like newel posts, like pawns guarding the queen.

The stillness was eerie.

Liz took her pencils and sketchbook from her pocket and sat on the edge of the lawn. She glanced round to make sure no one was looking, then began to draw the statue.

It was difficult, and when she had finished there was something sinister about her picture. It was there in the garden, but it fell like a shadow across the page. The statue looked almost alive – without thinking, Liz had given her arms and hands – and the chessmen weren't guarding her. They were keeping her in, like a pale prisoner.

She drew two figures peering at the statue from behind one of them, and that made the picture even more sinister. The prickly feeling came back along her arms as beneath the drawing she wrote some words. Now the story she was making held a meaning, like a riddle.

"The stranger took her to the topiary garden and showed her a woman turned to stone," she read aloud, very quietly.

"Aye, that's just about the sum of it," said a dry voice and a real shadow fell across the page.

Liz jumped and scrambled to her feet.

It was Sally Beck, still in her coat and wellingtons, smiling at her. She looked even older than she had done the night before. Beneath her cloth cap, her face was like a crumpled brown paper bag.

"I was looking for me dad!" said Liz.

"Were you heck-as-like!" said the old woman, and chuckled. "You come sneaking in that gate like a fox into a hen-coop!"

"Well, I only wanted to see."

"You writing a story?" The old woman jerked her chin towards the sketch-pad.

"I was just drawing a picture. I wasn't doing no harm."

"Any fool can see that," said Sally Beck. "You want a cup of tea?"

Liz nodded. "Yes, please."

"Grand. I just fancied a good natter. And I'll tell you something for nothing, lass, you look a sight more cheerful than you did last night."

"I was a bit fed up then," said Liz, as she walked slowly along with the old woman.

"Just reminded me of meself, you did. Leaning on that gate, scowling at the world. Sally, I says to meself when I saw you, there's another Jack Beck if ever I saw one."

They went round the side of the Hall, through a gate, and into a wilder rougher part of the garden where there was a big vegetable patch, a long greenhouse, and a small wooden shed.

"They always leave me a tin of tea in the shed," said Sally Beck. "Like leaving a saucer of milk for an old cat."

"Do you work here, then?" asked Liz, as the old woman unlocked the shed door.

"Work here! I'll have you know – I was head gardener, me lass! Head of all this!" She swept her arm in a wide bony gesture across the Hall and its grounds. "Aye, yes, I was. It's too much for me now. I'm ninety-one, you know." She laughed and all the wrinkles of her face trembled. "Ninety-one! Yes. Yes, I am." Then she stopped laughing and looked at the key in her lumpy hand. Her fingers were like a bunch of twisted knobbly sticks. "Ninety-one," she said quietly. "Who would credit it?"

"That means," said Liz, reckoning it up, "that you'll be a hundred in nine years!" She'd never met anyone that old.

Sally Beck shook her head. "Pushing up daisies, more like." She stooped into the shed and fetched out a flask and a stained white mug. "You'll have to have yours out o't lid," she said. Then she lowered herself down onto a bench in the shade. "You pour it, lass. Me hands is all trembles."

Liz did as she asked. It wasn't like being with a stranger at all. She knew that was partly because she had drawn the old woman twice in her book, and although the drawings were not realistic like photographs, anyone who looked at them would have been able to recognise Sally Beck, from the stick and the cap, and the sharp humpy shoulders.

"Eh," sighed the old woman as Liz handed her the mug. "It's not all a bed of roses."

"What isn't?"

"Being ninety-one. Head full of cobwebs – just like this old shed. It's your faculties, see. Full of cobwebs and rusty old things. Aye, it's your faculties. They get rusty after a lifetime int' rain . . ." She sucked her tea noisily from the rim of the mug, "and all the folks that were your friends and your foes are all dead and done, until there's only theesen." Sally Beck's voice was like the rattle of leaves along a gravel path. "I wasn't always old like this, lass. But there's nobbut me and Him minds the time when I looked like you."

They were silent for a long moment. The hot sky rippled

like silk above the trees, and the faint roar of the motorbikes on the fell was like the tearing of cotton.

Liz said, "It sounds a bit lonely."

"Lonely?" Sally Beck nodded. Her neck wobbled under her chin. "Aye, it's lonely. Sometimes. Makes you feel like a ghost sometimes . . ."

"You looked a bit like a ghost last night." Liz grinned, remembering the footsteps on the quiet lane.

"Give you a fright, did I?"

"Just for a minute," said Liz. Then she did something she rarely did. She pulled out her sketchbook and opened it for Sally Beck to see. "I drew you."

"Hold on." The old woman fumbled in her pocket for a pair of spectacles. She took the sketchbook and held it close to her face. She did not say anything. After a time she turned the page and looked at the other two drawings. "You did these, lass?" Round her mouth the lines trembled like dusty cobwebs.

Liz nodded. She watched the old woman's lips move silently as she read the words to herself. The quiet of the garden surged round them, and through the archway in the hedge Liz could see the shadow of the statue lying like a sundial across the lawn.

"That's a strange story you're writing," said Sally Beck at last.

"Oh," said Liz. Her face felt hot. "It's not really a proper story . . ."

Sally Beck unhooked the spectacles from her ears and looked at Liz from under the shadow of her cap. "Now, this here," she pointed to the first picture Liz had drawn. "This might have been Jack Beck. That's to say, me. Ont' day I became Jack Beck." The way she said it, it sounded more like the beginning of an argument than the beginning of a story.

"Did you really mean it, then? About you being a boy?" Liz stared at her.

"Certainly! Certainly, I did. It's God's honest truth I'm telling you, me lass!" said Sally Beck indignantly. "Eh, and by the road, it isn't 'Red at night is my delight' – it's 'shepherd's delight.' "

"I know. But I liked it better my way," Liz said.

"Do you want me to tell you this story or don't you?"

"Yes!"

"Well, stop interrupting us then. And pour us the rest of me tea."

3

SALLY RAN. The shadows of the houses striped her and between the terraces flashed the early morning sun. "Clack-clack-clack" went her clogs on the cobbles and the echo of them rang from the walls of Holyroyd Mill.

"I can hear that sound now, ringing in me ears, like someone was after me."

"Clack-clack-clack" through the empty streets, scattering the sparrows and jackdaws from their pickings on the road. But already she could hear the "clitter-clat, clitter-clat" of the other clogs as all through the streets of Holyroyd, men and women made their way from the houses to the cotton mill.

It was the morning after her twelfth birthday, and she had run away. And by the time Saint Peter's struck six o'clock on that July morning Sally Beck was already on top of Holyroyd Hill with the bundle of stolen clothes and a loaf of bread clutched to her chest.

" 'If tha'll not get in service, tha'll get int' mill till tha's wed an' ah can wash me hands o' thee, Sally Beck – now get me supper.' That's what me Dad said on me twelfth birthday. That's all the present I got."

Sally kept running until the mill chimney was hidden by

the rise of the moor. Then she took off her skirt and her apron and her shawl and shoved them into a hole in the bottom of a dry-stone wall. It felt like the first time her arms and legs had ever seen the sun. She unrolled the bundle of clothes she had stolen off the end of the bed she shared with her brother Jack and her sister Alice. They were Jack's clothes she had pinched, and she put them on – trousers, and a shirt cut down from an old one of her dad's, brown waistcoat and white muffler. With a knife she had stolen from the kitchen, she sawed off her plaits. "And they lay like two brown snakes on the ground."

Up on the moors the wind blew cold on her bare neck. She pulled her brother's cap onto her head. Then, with tl.e loaf of bread tucked in her shirt, she walked off over the moor, following green sheep paths through the heather, looking for a road. She was up on the moors for three days, without seeing another soul, and at night she slept by the walls. She was twelve. "I was that hungry I tried to eat some grass, but when I picked a blade it left two streaks down me finger and thumb – because of the soot from the chimney of Holyroyd Mill, and all t'other mills in the valleys round.

"And at night I was that frit – I thought sheep would grow long teeth in the dark and come and eat me when I slept!"

Three days after she had run away, Sally met a man sitting by a little fire at the side of a white moorland road. Next to him was a cart, and a horse picketed out on a long rope. He was cooking some eggs in a tin over his fire, and in his hand he held a piece of cheese, and he was eating lumps of the cheese off the blade of his knife. But he never cut his tongue.

[33]

"I can't rightly remember what he said, that man. I come out of the heather and just stood staring at the cheese, and he give us some in the end. But he must have asked me name, because I told him me name was Jack Beck – that was me brother whose clothes I had on."

Sally was thin – she had always been thin. But after three days sleeping rough on the moor, she was thinner than ever. And the man did not guess that the boy who leaned against his cartwheel was really a girl.

In the back of the cart were slabs of grey stone settled in straw. They didn't have any words carved on them, but Sally knew at once what they were. She had seen stones like that in Saint Peter's churchyard. And when she sat on one of them in the jolting cart, she could not decide whether it was better or worse sitting on a grave-stone that had no name on it. A stone without a name was somebody's future, while any stone with a name on it was somebody's past.

The carter took her over the Pennines. He was a brown sour-faced man with a big black moustache. He didn't speak much – except to his horse. But he was kind in a rough way – sharing his meals. And it was him who taught her the name of her first flower – Death Come Quickly. "Herb Robert, most folks call it now – a little pink thing with ferny leaves." She had banged her arm on the side of the cart one morning, and he picked it and rubbed it on the bruise.

"That's a fine finicky hand for a lad, Jack," he said, holding her wrist.

"I've been badly," said Sally, snatching her hand away.

The man looked at her for a long time, chewing his

moustache thoughtfully. Then he shrugged.

Sally was sure he had guessed. He never said a word. But that night he put his jacket over her to keep her warm, and in the morning he went over a wall to relieve himself, instead of going against the hub of the cartwheel as he had done before.

Late that afternoon they came down off the moors, onto a lane beneath the whispering branches of tall trees. Sally slipped quietly off her grave-stone in the back of the cart. The man did not notice, because he was busy with the horse and the wooden brake, going so steeply downhill. She hid behind the gate post of a field until the very last sound of hooves and cartwheels had faded away.

She had no idea where she was – only that it was a long way from Holyroyd. When she stood up, the first thing she saw was the grey chimneys and gables of a big house among the trees, and the sun sitting on its tower like a blazing weather vane.

"Carlton Hall!" said Liz, sitting up and rubbing her elbow which had gone stiff from leaning.

"Aye. It was. But I didn't know that then. Any road up, who's telling this story? Thee or me?"

"Thee! I mean, you!"

"Well hold your noise, lass. You'll muddle me faculties. Now, where was I?"

"Carlton Hall."

"Oh, aye. Well now, at that time the head gardener was a chap called Samuel Cumpsty."

Sally had been standing with her head pressed between the railings of the wrought-iron gate for a long time before the man noticed her. He was an elderly man with a big stomach and thin legs. He had a face like a turnip, fringed with white side-burns. And he was standing on a pair of wooden steps, clipping away at a green bobbin of a bush, in a garden that looked as if it were made out of green bobbins and spools and newel posts. It was the strangest garden Sally had ever seen, but she could tell the bobbins were really only dense bushes and trees, because green clippings lay scattered all over the gravel path.

At last the man turned round on the steps, sat on them, took a stone from his pocket and began to sharpen the blades of the shears, stroking the stone along the blades with a long hissing whisper. For a time he frowned at the boy at the gate. Then he put the stone back in his waistcoat pocket. "You looking for something, lad?"

"Aye," said Sally Beck. "I'm looking for a job of work."

"And what line of a trade are you in?" said the man as he began clipping at the bush again. "Begging or thieving, I'll wager, by the look on you."

"I am not!" said Sally. The sun was going down behind the grand house, and the shadows of the gate were lying over the lane. "Fetching and carrying – I can do that."

"Oh aye," said the man, without looking round. "And can you say your prayers?"

"Our Father which art in Heaven hallowed be thee name," said Sally, very quickly.

"Fetching and carrying, is it?" The man straightened up

and pushed back his cap. "Well, fetch us that broom and carry them clippings to yon pile."

"And that was how I got me first job. As it turns out, his last lad had died of lock-jaw. Mr Cumpsty, I had to call him, and he called me Jack. And going through those big black gates was like going through the gates of heaven itself."

Sally Beck and Samuel Cumpsty worked until it was dark. Not a leaf or a twig was to be left on the gravel from his clipping, and although he had spread sacks under the bushes, it still took a long time to clear up. The moon was high by the time they had finished. And it was by moonlight that they raked smooth the gravel among the topiary trees.

Mr Cumpsty took her back to his cottage and, that night, for the first time in her life, Sally had a bed to herself. And, what's more, she had a mug of ale to put her to sleep.

The next morning he took her to the Hall, and it was there that Sally learned that all the hiring and firing was done by a man called Harrison, who wore white gloves. "He was only a servant to Sir William like the rest of the staff, but he thought he was God Almighty hisself! I thought he was the Devil – all in black, with a thin nose, and white hands. Even Sam Cumpsty had to take off his cap and hold it in front of him when he talked to that man." Harrison merely glanced at Sally, and wrote the name "Jack Beck" in a black book.

"It wasn't until four years later that I met the man I was working for – Sir William Chadwick . . . But I haven't come to that bit yet."

And so Sally became Jack, the gardener's lad, at Carlton Hall.

"And do you know, lass, the thing I remember most – the thing that was me freedom? Aye, daft it'll sound, but me freedom was being able to walk through the garden, with me hands in me pockets, whistling. Whistling! You see, it was like this then – in Holyroyd there was a saying,

'A whistling woman and a crowing hen
Brings bad luck to gentlemen.'

And if a lass was heard whistling, she'd get a clout. But Jack Beck could whistle to his heart's content – long as he was at his job, mind."

"But weren't you scared you'd be found out?" said Liz. The shadow of the statue had crept out of sight across the lawn.

"Scared! I was witless! Witless scared, sometimes. And at night I'd lie in me little bed, listening to Samuel Cumpsty snoring over me head, and an owl moaning in the trees, and I'd think on me brothers and sisters what I'd left. Till thinking made me cry some nights. Aye, that it did. But I wasn't for going back. I'd got something none of me sisters had – a bed I didn't have to share with anyone else; not with a sister, or a babby, or a husband . . . You'll not understand that, lass . . ."

"But what about your mam?" said Liz, thoughtfully, "Didn't you miss her?"

"She was passed missing," said the old woman. "Her name was on one of them stones in Saint Peter's churchyard when I was eight. There were nine live children in me family when I ran from Holyroyd. And three dead ones. And the last of those dead ones was a little lad who came feet first and kicked himself and me mam to death with the birthing of him."

"Topiary," said Sam Cumpsty, wiping his forehead on his sleeve, "is the Devil's own art!"

"How do you mean, Mr Cumpsty?" asked Sally. She had been at Carlton Hall three years and had still managed to keep her secret – but it was getting harder every day. Cumpsty's Tail, the Hall staff had nick-named the thin lad who spent all his time with the old gardener. But on the whole they thought well enough of Jack. He was hardworking, shy, kept himself to himself, they said.

"Well, you reckon it up, Jack," said Sam, coming down the stepladder. He sat on the edge of the lawn, the shears across his knees. He reached for the jug of cider they had left in the shade and tilted it on his arm to drink. Then he wiped his mouth, and continued, "Eight weeks every year it takes us to clip this lot – two whole months back and front of every summer. By the time you've been here six years – you'll have spent one whole year of your natural born days, clip-clipping these feckless articles!"

He passed the cider jug to Sally.

"I'll tell you something, Jack lad – when you get to my age you get to doing a bit of philosophising."

"What?"

"Thinking, Jack! Thinking! Using what's between your ears for more than keeping your cap on!"

"Oh," said Sally. Her arm ached from wielding the heavy shears. They were working on a yew tree that had been

grown and clipped and wired to the shape of an egg-timer. "What have you been thinking, Mr Cumpsty?"

"I've been thinking that topiary's the Devil's own art. That's what. I've been thinking of all the years of me four-score and ten that I've spent turning what's natural into what's unnatural, just for the pleasing of a gentleman's eye . . . Look at that yew – it should be a fine big churchyard tree by now. But oh no – our Sir William wants a wasp-waist of a useless article!"

Sally eyed their work. "It's like putting a tree in corsets," she said thoughtfully.

Sam Cumpsty laughed and slapped his knee. "Aye! It is that, Jack! Putting Mother Nature into corsets and stays – that's our job in the topiary garden. And all so that Sir William can glance up from his table and see her displayed for his pleasure!"

"Is that why they've put Liddy in corsets, do you reckon, Mr Cumpsty?" said Sally, as they walked back across the gravel path. Liddy was a maid at the Hall – a girl of about Sally's own age. And a week ago she had changed shape, from being soft and plump to being an egg-timer.

Sam laughed again. "Aye, it's much the same thing." Then he frowned. "Here, don't you go making fresh with young Liddy, Jack."

"Oh, I shan't do that, Mr Cumpsty," said Sally, and blushed for reasons that Samuel Cumpsty couldn't even have guessed.

Seeing Jack with a scarlet face, Sam smiled. "Aye, you're a good lad. Now hand us them shears."

[42]

"I thought to meself – there's more topiary going on in this garden than you've mind of, Samuel Cumpsty!"

It wasn't just Liddy up at the Hall who was changing shape. Sally was as well. And it was getting harder to disguise the fact. She felt safe enough in the garden, and in her small room at Sam's cottage which she shared with the garden-forks and spades and a terrier called Nelson. But the garden wasn't the only place she and Sam worked. Once a fortnight they were lent to the church down at Carlton Beck, to scythe the grass and trim the graves, and even to dig graves sometimes if the vicar's man was ill.

And, during the hay-making and the harvest they were expected to give a hand on the estate's farms.

"You see, lass, it wasn't that I wanted to be a boy in me nature or me body – I just wanted to be Sally Beck. Not Jack. But Sally Beck with Jack's freedom – do you follow? But I was getting so as I had to tie a bit of cotton rag tightly round me chest to stop them showing through me shirt and waist-coat. And once a month it was harder still . . . I knew in me bones that it couldn't go on. Those three years had been the happiest of me life. But I knew in me bones it was coming to an end – or to put it more basic, I knew in me hips and me bosom."

While the lads on the farms were growing their first fluffy beards, and their voices were going cracked high and low, "like the mouse-eaten bellows on the organ at Carlton Beck", Cumpsty's Tail was smooth-faced and, not so much thin, as willowy.

"I took some teasing that summer, lass, I can tell you. And

[43]

I was that fond of old Sam, and that frit on him finding out, that I often lay awake all night, thinking I should run away again. And the worse teasing of all was from that Liddy."

Every morning Sally had to go to the Hall kitchen to take an order from Mrs Baxter, the cook, for the vegetables she wanted for the day. Sam and Jack Beck grew most of the vegetables in a walled garden behind the Hall – there was even a peach tree growing against a south-facing wall, that was Mr Cumpsty's pride and joy.

" 'Now then, Jack, I want a couple of them nice onions, and some carrots, and I'll have a big basket of strawberries. Nice ones mind – his Lordship's got guests this evening. Oh, and what else? Aye, some bay-leaves and some rosemary for the lamb.' And Mrs Baxter would give me a big wicker basket, and, sometimes an oat cake or a bit of fruit cake – whatever she was baking."

But Liddy was often there as well, dressed in her black uniform and white collar, trying to pinch Jack's cap as he went through the door, or singing softly under her breath.

"What ails
Cumpsty's Tail
Can't grow a beard
So I've heard!"

"I died a thousand deaths going in that kitchen, lass, I had this feeling that Liddy would find me out – which she did in the end, in a manner of speaking . . . Eh, poor Liddy . . ."

"What happened?" said Liz. The shadow of the Hall had crept over them. And now the garden was very still. All the visitors had left, and the sound of motorbikes had died away to a summer evening's silence.

The old woman was staring at the ground, seeing something there that Liz could not see, but she could imagine. Another summer, over seventy years ago. The last summer of Jack Beck's whistling, with his hands in his pockets, in the topiary garden.

One Friday in late July a message came from the sexton at Carlton Beck. There was a grave to be dug for a young lad who had died on a local farm, gored by a bull. And the regular grave-digger was ill.

Samuel Cumpsty had woken that morning with a bad stomach, and he grumbled all the way to the churchyard, which was a three mile walk, although his stomach grumbled louder.

It was a hot day, and their boots were covered with dust by the time they got there. The grave was to be dug by the churchyard wall, far from the cool shadow of the black yew trees which grew by the lych-gate. The ground was stony and parched hard.

First they had to cut off the turfs which would be put back over the grave after the lad was buried. Sally did that, cutting neat squares with the blade of her shovel, and stacking the turf by the wall. But that was the easy part.

Then came the picking and the shovelling.

"Here," groaned Sam, at last. "You dig it Jack, and I'll lie in it."

"Eh, Mr Cumpsty," said Sally, leaning on her spade, up to

her waist in the hole. "Don't say that!" The sweat was running down her back and her ribs. More than anything in the world at that moment, she wanted to take off her shirt. But she daren't even take off her waistcoat.

"I'll tell you, Jack," said Sam Cumpsty, dabbing at his face with his handkerchief. "If I dig yon grave, it'll be me last. And if that blighter of a grave-digger was here, I'd belt him over the head with me shovel – then he'd know what it was like to feel badly! I'm telling you, lad! If that blighter's ill today it'll be because he's had a jug too many at the Carlton Arms!"

Sally grinned. But then she looked at old Sam. His face was like melting butter in the hot sun, ". . . and he was holding himself stiff, like. All crooked. He was in no state for digging a grave – save his own. And it scared me."

"Mr Cumpsty," said Sally, "you get on back to the cottage. I can finish up here. I've done it before. I promise – it'll be the tidiest bit of digging this side of Carlton Fell."

"I've mind to take your advice, lad," said Sam.

"Where there's a mind there's a will, Mr Cumpsty. I'll dig it right, don't you fret."

Sam nodded. He put his jacket back on, and pulled his cap out of his pocket to cover his balding head from the sun.

"You're a grand lad," he said. "And that poor soul you're digging grave for was same age as you. Think on. The vicar'll have a sermon out of your digging, I warrant."

Sally was left alone in the graveyard, among the urns and angels of the gentry and farmers, and the grey stones which cast their shadows over the green mounds of poorer folk.

It took her all afternoon to dig that hole. Until she was stood at the bottom, with the planks of wood shoring the sides to stop them caving in on her and burying her alive. She was fifteen, rising sixteen, and above her was a hot blue rectangle of sky. "I was that tired when it was done – I just lay down on the cool earth at the bottom of the grave. I pulled me cap over me eyes, and the next thing was – I was fast asleep."

When Sally woke, the moon was up. A sickle moon, above the squat tower of the church. For a second she could not remember where she was. She got stiffly to her feet and was about to climb out of the grave, when she heard a whisper and a giggle.

She stopped still, listening, afraid. But these weren't ghosts she was hearing. She recognised the laugh and the giggle – it was Liddy, the maid from the Hall. And, a moment later, she recognised the other voice – it was a labourer on one of the estate's farms. "Handsome as the Devil, he was. And married, with two little children and another one coming."

"I love you, Liddy," she heard him murmur. "Be kind to me, lass. Oh, be kind to me . . ."

Sally contemplated jumping out of the grave and giving them both a scare. But, instead, she crawled quietly out of the hole. Liddy and the labourer were not in the graveyard at all, but in the field over the wall. And now there were no voices, but sighs and gasps.

As quietly as she could, Sally collected up the shovels and the pick, and crept away through the grave-stones. Once she was out on the lane, she ran.

When she got back to the cottage, Sam was sitting in a chair outside the door, drinking a glass of sherry with an egg in it, that Mrs Baxter had brought down for him.

"Is it done?" he asked.

"Aye," said Sally. "I've made it neat, and it's all shored up. I fell asleep, Mr Cumpsty."

"Here," said Mrs Baxter, who was standing next to the chair. "Have you seen our Liddy?"

"No," Sally lied. But her voice made it sound like a lie. And both Mrs Baxter and Mr Cumpsty heard.

"Well," said Sam, handing his glass back to the cook. "There's no harm in seeing, is there?"

"That depends," said Mrs Baxter. "That depends."

By October, Liddy had changed shape again. And the labourer, his wife and three small children had gone. They went by night. No one ever saw them again.

It was Harrison who came for Sally. She was up in an apple tree in the orchard, tossing down apples to old Sam.

"Jack Beck?" said Harrison, as if her name wasn't worth the spittle he used in his saying it. "Sir William wants a word with you."

"Me?" Sally swung from a branch and landed in the soft grass.

"Harrison marched me off, as if I was to be hanged. And there was nothing Sam Cumpsty could do but stare, with a basket of apples in his arms."

As they crunched up the gravel path, Harrison never said

a word. But Sally knew, before they entered the panelled library, that Jack Beck's time was up. Someone had found out. She wanted the floorboards to open up and swallow her. And yet, also, there was a sense of relief. She had a feeling that she would have to pay for those happy years she had had. But she was ready to pay for them. It was like dying, but it was better than running away.

Sir William Chadwick was smaller than Sally had imagined – only the size of ordinary people, in fact. And older. His wife, Lady Chadwick, had died before Sally had come to Carlton Hall, and his only son lived in the south. Sir William spent a great deal of time in London, and Sally had only seen him once or twice before – standing at the library window, or strolling through the gardens.

"I like to think of my servants as family," he said, and doodled on his blotting paper. Without lifting a hand or saying a word, he somehow sent Harrison away.

"I stood in front of his desk, with me cap in me hands, while he give us this long sermon about family and responsibility and loyalty. I could tell by the look on him that he was not enjoying lecturing me – but I didn't know what he were on about."

"Well, Beck? Speak up. There's no need to be afraid," said Sir William.

Sally just frowned at the polished floor, baffled and scared.

"Of course," said Sir William, looking uncomfortable, "Liddy has been given her notice. The question remains – what are we to do with you, Beck?"

Then, suddenly, it dawned on Sally what this interview

was about. Liddy was going to have a baby, and Sir William had been told that Jack Beck was the father of the child! "I just stood gawping at him. I couldn't believe me ears! Whatever possessed Liddy I'll never know – perhaps she was that shamed to admit she'd been with a married man. Or, more like, she wouldn't tell them the name of the man, and Mrs Baxter had remembered that night when I was late home from the churchyard. Any way up, I was in the queerest pickle. I knew I was about to get the sack.

"Sally, I thought to meself, you may as well be hung for a sheep as a lamb!"

Sir William was standing with his back to her, looking out of the library window over the topiary garden. His hands were behind his back, and he was tapping the two fingers of his right hand in the palm of his left.

"It wasn't me!" said Sally.

"I'd rather you didn't lie to me, Beck. It's a deuced bad business as it is."

Sally took a deep breath. "It can't have been me, Sir," she said.

Sir William turned, frowning. "Oh, and why not?"

"Because," said Sally in a whisper. "Me name's not Jack, Sir. It's Sally."

"Pardon?" Sir William stared at her.

"Me name's not really Jack, Sir. It's Sally. And I'm not a lad. I'm a lass."

There was a silence like thunder.

"I was shaking that much, I thought I was going to fall down. And Sir William looked as if he was going to fall down, and all! Any road, to cut a long story short, I was dragged off to the kitchen by Mrs Baxter, and made to take all me clothes off in front of her. I stood on the cold tiles as naked as a nail. And she was that overcome she burst into tears and blew her nose on her apron.

"Then there was that much conflabbing and consternation. They couldn't have been more shocked if Jack Beck had grown wings and flown away!

"Harrison was all for handing me over to the law, for fraud and deception. Well, I was given a skirt belonging to another maid to put on, and I was taken back to Sir William. I was that used to britches, I felt naked dressed like that . . . Any road, I spent all evening with his Lordship – sobbing, I was. And I had to tell him the story of me life." The old woman smiled at Liz.

And Liz was gazing at her, unaware that the shadows in the topiary garden had joined to a blue darkness.

"He let us stay on! I couldn't believe it. But he let us stay on, as a gardener! I wasn't to live at Sam Cumpsty's cottage any more – that wasn't decent now I was a lass! And I wasn't to work in the churchyard or in the fields. Of course there was a right scandal and Harrison tried to make life a torment until the day he died. But Sir William always had a kind word, and so did Mrs Baxter when she come round."

"But what about Samuel Cumpsty?" said Liz.

The old woman shook her head sadly. "He never spoke to me again. It wrung me heart, that did. And he died that winter of this cancer of his stomach. He'd been like a father to Jack . . . I could still weep when I think on . . . He was

[52]

buried down at Carlton Beck, and I always kept his grave nice, with flowers and that.

"They were going to employ a new gardener, but somehow they never got round to it. Then Kaiser's War came on and the whole world changed. By the time that was done, I was back at Sam Cumpsty's cottage as head gardener and Sir William – he was an old man in a bath-chair by then – often come down the garden for a talk. And when he died, he left it in his will that Sally Beck was to have the cottage to live in for the rest of her days. So here I've stayed.

"Now what do you think of that, me lass?"

Liz shook her head. "Didn't you miss being Jack?"

"Heavens, no!" cried Sally Beck. "Oh, I'd been happy then – but I was far happier being meself for the rest of me days! But I'll tell you something – I've still got Jack Beck's waistcoat and cap, and his leather leggings and boots. I just kept them for sentimentality, I suppose." The old woman held out her hand. "Here, lass. Give us a pull up. I've got stiff with sitting."

Liz jumped to her feet and helped haul her off the bench. It was getting darker. "You'd better run," said Sally Beck. "They lock the gates at nine."

"Oh heck!" cried Liz. "I was meant to be back for teatime!" She grabbed her sketchbook. "Thanks for telling me the story! I'll come and see you tomorrow."

"Aye, if you've a mind. I'm mostly in the garden, or at me cottage. Good-night, lass."

"Good-night!" cried Liz, and dashed away through the eerie shapes of the topiary trees.

[53]

4

DAD WAS FURIOUS. "I've got half the camp site looking for you!" It was a bit of an exaggeration.

"I'm sorry. I never noticed the time."

"Well, where the heck were you?"

"I was at the Hall, talking to the gardener."

"What did I tell you about talking to strange men! I might as well talk to a brick wall!"

"It wasn't a man. It was a woman, called Sally Beck. I am sorry, Dad. Honest, I am."

Dad sighed. "Well, at least you're safe. Now get in the caravan."

Shortly afterwards, Alan and his friend, Mike, came back.

"She's here," said Dad. "Now come on, let's get some supper on. My stomach thinks my throat's been slit!"

Soon, the smell of frying beefburgers and onions filled the caravan. Liz sat by the window, watching Dad cook, but she was thinking about Jack Beck.

"Well, aren't you going to ask?" said Dad.

"Ask what?" said Liz.

"If I won."

"Oh! Did you?"

"No. But I came third!" Dad grinned, very pleased with

himself, and forgetting that he was supposed to be angry with her.

"Great! Does that mean you win a prize?"

"No, but it means I qualify for tomorrow's event, and I'm in with a good chance. Do you want onions on your beefburger?"

"Yes, please."

Dad passed Alan and Mike a plate each. They were out in the awning, sharing a can of beer. Then he came and sat opposite Liz. "Have you thought any more about the fancy dress, Lizzy?"

Liz shook her head. She had forgotten all about it.

"Dad?" said Liz, as she poured herself a mug of tea. "You know when I said I'd been talking to the gardener – why did you think I meant a man?"

"I don't rightly know. It's just what you expect, I suppose . . ." Dad remembered he was angry again. "Now you listen to me, our Lizzy. When I say tea-time, I mean tea-time!"

"Yes, Dad."

Liz had a nightmare. She was in the topiary garden but now all the trees and bushes were really women, like the statue on the lawn. Green women, rooted to the soil.

And a man with a thin nose and white gloves was walking among them, snipping off their arms with a huge pair of shears. He came towards Liz, and she suddenly realised that she was a topiary woman as well. "S-nap! Ss-nap!" went his shears as he came at her.

And Liz jerked awake. Her face was wet with sweat, and

the sleeping bag was tied in a knot round her legs. Outside, it was light. She could hear Dad breathing softly at the other end of the caravan. And the awning was flapping in the cool dawn breeze. That was the sound she had heard in her dream.

She straightened the sleeping-bag and lay back down, but she could not get back to sleep. The dream was like a picture in her mind.

Soon it would be morning. It was getting lighter all the time. Dad turned onto his back and started to snore quietly in the back of his throat.

At last she got her sketchbook and pencils from the end of the bunk, and she tried to put the picture of her dream down on the page, until concentrating on the drawing made her fear go away. It was a weird picture – the topiary women were roughly sketched in, with long black shadows lying at their feet. And, for some reason, even those that had had their arms cut off still had them in their shadows.

In the centre of the picture she drew a man. He was thin, all dressed in black, wielding a huge pair of scissors, almost as big as himself. They were meant to be shears, but they looked more like scissors, and that made the picture weirder still. She thought he looked like the Devil, so she drew two tiny horns sticking out of his head, – but she didn't give him a tail.

Under the picture, she wrote *Topiary is the Devil's own art* which is what Samuel Cumpsty had said to Jack Beck.

Yawning, she began to colour in the sky, and, with her cheek resting on the page, she fell back to sleep.

LIZ RAN through the open gate and into the black shadows of the topiary trees. Then she stopped, disconcerted. It gave her an odd feeling being among the clipped bushes, so soon after her dream. It was like walking out of one room into another, and finding the same person seated in both.

On her wrist she was wearing Dad's watch. "Back at six," he had said, "or you'll miss the barbecue." She had still been in her sleeping bag when he and Alan set off up the fell, for the last trials' event of the weekend. They would be leaving tomorrow morning, early, because Dad had to be at work at the garage by nine.

She found the old woman sitting on the bench by the shed. At her feet was a big wicker basket containing a lumpy brown paper parcel, a bunch of radishes and a lettuce.

"Now then," said Sally Beck, "I've brought something to show you."

"I've got something to show you as well," said Liz, pulling her sketchbook out of her pocket.

Sally Beck chuckled. "You first then."

"I had a bad dream about the garden last night," said Liz, pulling her sketchbook out of her pocket. "Look, that's a picture of it."

The old woman put on her spectacles. "It looks like that devil, Harrison! It must have been a blooming bad dream!"

"That's who it's meant to be, I think."

"Here! I hope you're not going to hold me responsible for your dreams, lass!"

Liz laughed. "I shan't," she said. But she had a feeling that she would visit the topiary garden again in nights to come.

[58]

"I'm pleased to hear it," said Sally Beck. "Want a radish?"

"No, thanks, I've just had my dinner." Dad had left her a plate of sandwiches.

"Now then. You have a look in there." The old woman poked the brown paper parcel with the end of her stick.

Liz sat on the grass at her feet and untied the string, but she had already guessed what it contained. There was a strong smell of moth-balls.

Inside, there were a pair of brown boots, a cloth cap, a green waistcoat, and two pieces of leather fringed with buckles.

"Now then," said Sally Beck. "They're what you call 'leggings'. I give 'em a bit of a rub with lard this morning, to bring up the shine."

"Lard?"

"Aye. By rights it should be pig fat dubbin. Here, try them on. First put on the boots. Well, go on! They might not fit you, mind."

Reluctantly, Liz pulled off her sandals and tried on the boots. They were stiff and hard. The leather had cracked in places, but they were big enough. The eye-holes were newly threaded with pieces of string. She had a picture in her mind of Jack Beck lying at the bottom of the grave, looking up at the rectangle of twilight, hearing whispers and giggles. It was like putting on a dead person's clothes.

"Now, wrap leggings round your calf. No! T'other way up! Aye, that's right. Now, do up the buckles."

The buckles were rusty and stiff. They nipped her fingers, but at last she stood and looked down at her old-fashioned feet. "They're a bit like Dad's motorbike boots," she said. She looked at the waistcoat. It was faded, and there was a brown stain down the green satin back.

She did not want to put it on. She was afraid of something, but she wasn't sure what. Something daft – a daft fear that the clothes might whisk her back in time, like in a story, to a life of having to pretend to be something you were not. Of only being able to feel free by hiding what you really were with a tightly bound cotton rag and a waistcoat.

There was something daft and devilish about Sally Beck's story. Not in what she had done, which was brave, but in the fact that she had to do it at all.

But the old woman was smiling at her, wanting to see how she would look.

Liz put on the cap.

"No, pull it back. Here, let me do it." With her twiggy fingers she yanked the cloth cap on Liz's head. Then she took it off again. "Stick your plaits on your head."

Liz held up her hair, and Sally Beck pushed the cap firmly back.

Liz's ears felt naked, and her neck felt bare. She slipped the waistcoat over her T-shirt.

"Horn, them buttons," said the old woman as Liz fastened them. "Mrs Baxter used to buy them off this tinker chap . . ." She fell silent. She looked at Liz out of the dry crinkles of her face. Her own cap cast a black shadow across her eyes. Then she pulled a clean white handkerchief from her coat pocket. Liz leaned forward and the old woman knotted it round her neck.

[60]

They were both silent.

At last Sally Beck said, very quietly. "I was thinner and plainer than you, lass."

The silence went on.

"And I had two shirts – one for working, and one for best. And they both had buttons carved out of sea shells. Shirts you had to pull on over your head . . . Nearest I ever got to the sea, them little white buttons . . ."

Somewhere in the topiary garden a thrush was singing. And a jackdaw croaked on the tower of Carlton Hall with a sound like, "Tjack! Jack!" With a sound like a black laugh.

Liz did not need a mirror. She knew what the old woman was seeing from her shadowed eyes.

Funny, thought Liz. My name's Jackson. Jack's son . . . I wonder why there isn't a Jackdaughter?

She shook her head. It was like trying to wake up. Then she took off the cap. And the waistcoat and the boots and the leggings. She put them back in the paper, and tied up the parcel with string.

The old woman watched her. Her face was so dry and withered, Liz could not read her expression, any more than you could guess what a tree stump was thinking. But then she smiled, and nodded slowly.

Liz said, "Did you never go back to Holyroyd?"

"No," said Sally Beck. "I never did. I never saw me sisters or me brothers again. But I can guess where they'll be now. Under grey stones, lass. Under grey stones."

"Ninety-one . . ." said Liz, looking at her.

"Aye," said Sally Beck. "We're a long living breed us

women." She laughed very softly. "Gives us a chance to see the world change, lass. Yes. Yes, it does."

The bonfires for the barbecue were already glowing on the camp site field when Liz got back. The flames looked pale and small against the bright evening sky.

Dad and Alan were in the awning, laughing and writing signs saying "Laurel" and "Hardy" to hang round their necks, because you could not really tell who they were meant to be from the clothes they had on.

"Hello, our Lizzy!" said Dad. "Guess who came second?"

"Only the man himself!" said Alan, and pointed his finger at Dad's ear.

"That's great!" said Liz.

"Well, what are you going as?" Dad stuffed a cushion up his shirt to make him look fatter.

"Oh . . ." She had forgotten all about the Fancy Dress. She frowned and glanced round the camp site. There were laughs and shouts from the other caravans. A cowboy and a pirate were strolling over to the fire.

"Well?" said Dad.

A black bird flew across the pale rising moon, heading for the chimneys of Carlton Hall.

"Tjack! Jack!"

"Oh," said Liz. "I think I'll just go as myself."